Stories to Read by Candlelight

by Jean Lorrain

Translated by Patricia Worth

Illustrated by Erin-Claire Barrow

Published by Ensorcellia,
an imprint of Odyssey Books, in 2019

Copyright © Patricia Worth 2019
Illustrations Copyright © Erin-Claire Barrow 2019

www.odysseybooks.com.au

A Cataloguing-in-Publication entry is available from the National Library of Australia

ISBN: 978-1-925652-58-1 (pbk)
ISBN: 978-1-925652-59-8 (ebook)

Cover design: Simon Critchell

The following stories from this collection
have previously been published:

'Madame Gorgibus': *The Brooklyn Rail
'in Translation'*, February 2015

'Princess Mandosiane': *Eleven Eleven*, Issue 19

'Queen Maritorne': *Eleven Eleven*, Issue 19

'Gudule the Maid': *Danse Macabre*, 99

'Useless Virtue': *Sun Star Review*, Vol 1, Issue 2

Introduction

About forty years ago in the little old towns of the bourgeoisie and the judges, in the homes of the old families, one could meet neat and discreet little people treated less as hirelings than as friends. They did not live in the attic but spent at least three or four days a week relegated to the family's upstairs linen room, laboriously occupied, the darling creatures, in works of sewing and mending for the household.

These young seamstresses, these wenches with a needle, *cousettes* as they were rudely and impertinently named in the eighteenth century to which they seemed to belong, were the joy of every provincial childhood, today mature and in their forties.

They were spinsters, somewhat sanctimonious, finicky and gossipy, yet our parents would not have suffered them being ridiculed in church. They were trusted to take children to their grandparents' homes, where in a large room cluttered with armoires these sweet old girls would bring their strangely thoughtless heads together and tell gripping stories.

They had no end of odd habits: mass at six in the morning that they wouldn't miss for anything in the world; the pot of embers dying beneath ashes that they lugged around in all weathers—rain, snow, and wind squalls—shielding it under a corner of their mantle; the most stubborn refusal to take a place at a table where cutlery was crossed; curious devotions and little faïence saints that they always kept buried at the bottom of some huge pocket under their skirts; a priceless way of crossing themselves at any swearword; and hair-splitting, and fussmaking, and curtseying!

I knew one of these poor, pitiable girls. Her name was Norine; she came to my grandmother's during the day and was responsible for all the mending work in the house. She had once been pretty and had a suitor with honourable intentions, but Norine never wanted to leave her old, infirm parents. One fine morning the lover grew tired of waiting, and Norine grew old alone in her little worker's cottage with the memory of her old parents who had died late in life, and perhaps with regret for the lover who had left. In my grandmother's house Norine was greatly loved; she was an old maid with funny ways, though she was upright, honest, and would never lie. But I sense melancholy descending and filling me as I try to recall this colourless and frail little figure; all the ashes of the past are blanketing these stories in a premature snow, and I wanted them to be cheerful. I've drifted unwittingly into the inexpressible charm of this small autumnal town, this small fortified town like an etching from the last century, the kind of town with a belfry, trees in quincunx arrays and, in the market, tall houses with sculpted gables.

Brr! Brr! Brr!

'But anyway,' as Norine herself would say, 'a pinch of tobacco and a demitasse of coffee, and with that we can thumb our nose at the devil.'

Here is the first of Norine's stories, such as she would tell it in her rather peculiar language, when the girls—my cousins—and I would gather round her knees in my grandmother's linen room.

Monsieur d'Avonancourt

'Now, then! My chattering little ladies, and you, sir, awake after your long sleep, let me tell you about a rich and powerful lord, a marquis and Grand Cordon, Monsieur du Tillet d'Avonancourt. He had lived a long time in Paris and also in Versailles, where he had done some things which were not nice, they say, for this happened under Louis XV, before that beggar of a Revolution. In those towns he had often visited people of all sorts, bankers and alchemists, in fact, many types more in favour with hell than with the Church. He had, they say, been present at the *Great Work*. What it was, the local people would have been hard-pressed to say, but it was ...' (and here Norine always crossed herself) '... the final abomination.

'So it was that when he returned to this region, on his last legs and at a loss for words, no one in the nobility cared to see a man as compromised as he. They said he was more dead than alive. But the little vidame[1] of Ravanailles could not stand this; as a child, he had been acquainted with the old marquis in his father's house. So one morning, consumed by curiosity, he left for the house of du Tillet.

'It was mid-autumn, the plane trees were already yellow, and on the lawns were dead spots resembling twenty-franc coins. He arrived at the entrance to the park, made enquiries at the gate, and with a lively leap from his Berlin, stopped, agog and astounded, his mouth agape, to learn that Monsieur le Marquis, whom he believed to be in bed and yielding up his ghost, was taking a walk round the park. In he dashed, and at the end of the most majestic avenue what do you think he saw? Straight as a post, head held high, gold-knobbed cane in his hand, the old Marquis d'Avonancourt in person.

'This man, spry as a youth, saw the vidame

1.　Vidame: the deputy of a bishop in temporal affairs.

in the distance and called out to him. In a falsetto voice, his fist proudly planted on his hip, he said:

'"Well, well! Vidame, you coming to see if I'm dead? In town they're barking lustily about my last gasp. You can see that I'm in quite good health, eh! eh! I'm taking a turn round the park and I'm not afraid of the cool air!"

'And in a singularly cutting tone, he continued:

'"And there are no clergy, no doctors in my house. What need do I have of that lot? I'm doing very well, you must admit, for my seventy years, young man!"

'And, with an authoritative blow of his cane, he struck the ground littered with dead leaves and said:

'"I come here every evening to take my turn round the park; the sunsets here are splendid, you must admit. I'm here this evening and I'll come on many more evenings yet; and those money-lenders bothered by this, I'll tell them myself, straight to their faces, eh! eh! eh!"

'The vidame of Ravanailles has since told how he then had a strange sensation of malaise. The marquis had suddenly seemed to him so oddly thin on that autumnal crepuscular avenue that a little graveyard chill descended on him. This haughty, sarcastic silhouette profiled in black against the crimson sky reminded him alarmingly, with its very smile and its sunken, gleaming eyes, of a certain Monsieur de Voltaire, a heathen in the manner of Monsieur le Marquis and no better than him.

'The vidame took his leave rather hastily without that great rogue of a marquis troubling to escort him. Quickly, quickly, he got back to his Berlin and called out:

'"Hup! Don't spare the horses! A big tip for the postilion!"

'And at full gallop he reached the town's ramparts where the first news he heard on arrival at the gates was that the marquis had been dead since the previous day.

'And the vidame had just seen him, had just spoken to him. And this chateau, visited by death, this chateau of a dream, this phantasmagoric chateau where unreal valets and ghosts had received him...!

'"I come here every evening to take my turn round the park; the sunsets here are superb, you must admit. I'm here this evening and I'll come back on many more evenings yet."

'The vidame had a quartan fever and took forthwith to his bed. And,' added good old

Norine with a frightful, contrite expression, 'the worst was that this evil man, the marquis, kept his word; he continued to take a walk in court dress, the gold-knobbed cane in his hand, along his avenue lined with plane trees. Twenty years ago, people were still meeting him there.'

And Norine would cite names of people she had known, which proves, she concluded, by way of an evangelical moral, that evil is for all time and the devil never dies.

We didn't really understand, I confess, how the marquis, who was dead, could take a walk in his park and chat with the vidame, and even a hundred years later could still be coming back. But we were thrillingly moved, and with all our little hearts pounding we shuddered at Norine's mysterious intonations and alarming pauses. She was a marvellous storyteller because she fascinated her listeners; she believed in what she was telling, and that's the secret. And when she had finished jabbering on with her mad ideas, we would say:

'Again, Norine, again!'

You can't expect more from a story.

Tales for Sick Children

These are tales for the ill, tales for the heavy air of bedrooms with herbal teas and hot infusions, tales to be told between six and seven, the hour when fever increases, when Norine was invited to come and dreamily tell stories at our much-loved childhood bedside.

She would tiptoe into the deepening shadows of the bedroom, slipping in without a sound and sitting down at the head of our little bed. And in her toneless voice she would begin:

I

Princess Mandosiane

Princess Mandosiane was six hundred years old. For six centuries she had lived embroidered onto velvet, her face and hands painted on silk. She was dressed all in pearls, her gorget rippling with heavy beading, and her gown was woven with threads of argentite and arabesques of the finest gold.

A mantle of ultramarine sown with sprays of anemones was fastened to her chest with precious gemstones, and sapphire cabochons finished the hem of her gown.

For a long time she had figured in processions and royal celebrations. She would be brought out and hoisted up on a banner staff, and the dazzle of her jewels would bring joy to great ladies and commoners. They were happy times when the streets would be hung with flags and flickering flamboyant bunting, and the people would cheer for Princess Mandosiane. Then she would be returned ceremoniously to the cathedral treasury and shown to strangers in exchange for much gold.

She was a wonderwork, this miraculous

princess, born of the dream and the untiring work of twenty nuns who laboured for fifty years to form the exquisite, hieratic figure from skeins of silk and silver threads.

Her hair was of yellow silk; two tourmaline crystals of the most beautiful blue were inlaid for irises; and she held a lily branch of white velvet which lay over her heart.

Then the era of processions passed, thrones were abolished, kings disappeared, civilisation marched on, and the princess of pearls and painted silk now remained confined in the shadow and silence of the cathedral.

There she spent her days in the twilight of a crypt amid a pile of bizarre things grimacing in the corners: there were old statues, rich goblets beside ciboria and old church ornaments, copes still stiff and seeming to shimmer with sunlight but which were slowly fading away in the darkness with the chalices that no longer served sacramental wine.

There was also an old statue of Christ in a corner, his back to the wall, veiled in spider webs. The door of the underground chapel was never opened anymore; all these old things were sleeping, buried there and forgotten, and Princess Mandosiane felt a great despair in her heart.

Now, she lent her ear to the counsel of the red

mouse, an insidious little mouse, fast as lightning, persistent and wilful, who had haunted her for years.

'Why stubbornly remain a captive, armour-plated in all these pearls and embroidery holding you so tightly? Yours is not a life, you have never lived, not even during the times when you sparkled on those fine days of proclamations and pealing bells, cheered on by euphoric crowds, and now, you see, your life is oblivion, it is death. If you like, with my sharp teeth I could undo one by one the stitches of silk and gold cord that have held you in place for six hundred years, motionless in this lustrous velvet which, just between us, has lost its brilliance. It will perhaps hurt a little, especially when I unpick the stitches close to your heart, but I'll begin with the long contours, those of your hands and your face, and already you will be able to stretch and move, and you will see how good it is to breathe and to live! Beautiful as you are, with the face of a fairy-tale princess and rich with the fabulous treasures of your resplendent gown, you will be dressed by the greatest tailors, and you will be taken for a banker's daughter and will marry no one less than a French prince.

'All over you, there are gemstones worth millions. Come! Let me set you free, you will revolutionise the world. If you only knew how good it is to be free, to breathe deeply in the fresh air and to pursue your only fantasy! You are clad in these opals and sapphires like a knight in armour and you have never even fought in battle. I know some paths that lead to the land of happiness. Let yourself blossom outside your corset of embroidery; we will travel the world together and I promise you a throne and a hero's love.'

And Princess Mandosiane consented: the little red mouse began his murderous task immediately; his teeth sawed, cut and filed into the moth-eaten velvet; pearls chinked as they fell one by one. On nights by the light of the moon and on days of beautiful sunshine, in the crypt illuminated by a small high window, the red mouse busily cut and gnawed.

When he attacked the famous gorget of nacre and pearls, Princess Mandosiane felt a sharp coldness in her heart.

For several days she had a sense of shivering, and felt lighter and singularly supple where all the stitches had been unpicked, and she swayed in the fabric as though animated by a breeze, and waited with delight for the mouse to finish his work.

As the devourer's teeth sank into her chest,

the poor princess of spangles and silk now came completely unstitched; it was like ash flowing over the flagstones in the darkened chapel, the soft fall of silk flakes and torn braids and luminous rags; a few cabochons rolled away like wheat grains and the shabby old velvet of the banner tore from top to bottom.

And that's how Princess Mandosiane died for having listened to the insidious counsel of a little mouse.

Among the stories that Norine would reel off when she came upstairs to nurse our fever, there were, occasionally, some that were rather extraordinary and more suited to overexciting an ailing mind than to appeasing a nervous child; but Norine did not mean any harm by them. She would tell her story such as she knew it, off the cuff, drawing it randomly from her repertoire, and we would have grieved the poor girl if we had told her that she had increased the fever of one of us.

Among these strange, gossipy tales there were two in particular which gave me goose bumps and made me jump straight into bed, pull the covers up to my chin and shiver with delight: the story of

Madame Gorgibus and the adventure of the maid Gudule.

I'll write them here for you.

II

Madame Gorgibus

Chapter One

Three white cats with ribbons on their necks are dancing round the cauldron. The fine milk is boiling, and one of them, now and then, carefully dips his claw in. But, oh! The greedy thing! And he scampers back with three leaps, yowling. Three white cats with ribbons on their necks are dancing round a cauldron.

The old raven, perched at the corner of the window, watches over them as in a dream, his eyes half-closed. Hard to know if he sleeps or wakes, the crestless raven, almost a hundred years old, perched at the corner of the window in the shadow of the curtains.

Perhaps he's dreaming of the great shimmering cypress and pine woods where in his youth he would fly swiftly, calling *crrruck! crrruck! crrruck!,* he and his sisters, my ladies the crows, deafening all the country round.

The old raven might also be dreaming of the cooler sky of April, when nests were built all through the tall budding trees, and were filled with chattering chicks, and that was joy, abundance, and love.

Ah! Why did the wretched woodcutter break his wing? A fine bit of mischief! A thrown stone, and now a sea of resentment swells the heart of the old bird.

On the mantelpiece there is a Dresden china figurine, an ancient little shepherdess with pink painted cheeks who for two hundred years has mimed the same greeting. Oh! How bored she must be, my goodness! There is also a figure of Christ in blue faïence from Quimper and an hourglass that is never turned over.

All these objects are velveted with dust: the Christ is the colour of ash, and the little old Dresden piece, shrouded in spider webs, despairs; oh, that frozen gesture of vainly shaking her crook and flounces.

As for the hourglass, it has fallen asleep. Besides, everything in this house is so old that the objects don't seem to remember what to do.

The old almanac hanging near the fireplace is

dated at least twenty-five years ago; some old etchings which could be by Holbein are fading away beneath their tarnished glass; the antique weight-driven clock in its waxed walnut case looks more like a sarcophagus; no tick-tocking nor mouse trotting in the dusty neglect of this old house.

The three white cats with ribbons on their necks are dancing round the cauldron, and the raven is devouring and ruminating his gall. Ah! Yet, when the wicked old fairy who lives in this lair comes back from her walk on the ramparts, it seems he would only have to muster courage and take one good leap; he would flutter about her face and stun her with pecks of his great beak, then he would wait until the old hag had quite fainted so he could peel her eyeballs at his leisure. Oh! With the end of his old beak he would dig into her eye sockets and peck out her old eyes. And the old raven feels his feathers puff out: he runs, he flaps his wings, he swells and fills with a savage pleasure, *crrruck, crrruck, crrruck.* Not with impunity did he have a few noble ancestors at the gibbet of Montfaucon. Noblesse oblige. But, click and frist, a key turns in the lock, someone has come into the lane, and Madame Gorgibus, wrapped in her puce ruched silk cape and capuche, enters the old dwelling. For her old raven (oh, how little she suspects the darkness of his soul!) she brings a piece of calf lung, and its smell disarms the shifty creature; then she heads for the fireplace and crouches down in the ashes with all her cats climbing after her.

'You've had enough, stop it, Blanchette, you'll get a beating! Babyface, if you want a clip on the ear ... !'

She tastes the milk, finds it just right, closes the inside shutter of the little window, puts My Lord Raven in his wicker cage and, over it, a piece of calico that will cast a shadow and put him to sleep. She lights her old green-shaded oil lamp, draws an old winged armchair close to the hearth and sits in it to take a nap before the evening supper.

The three white cats purr on her stomach, stretched out in the lovely warmth. Master Raven is asleep, a captive in his darkened cage.

Poor Madame Gorgibus, she won't be murdered yet, not tonight.

Chapter Two

The ways of Madame Gorgibus were a bit of a mystery. She was a little old stay-at-home, pretentious, and always got up in hooded cloaks, leafy fabrics

and feathered hats in last century's fashion, giving her a ridiculous air of Carnaval. She was a source of amusement for the urchins of the neighbourhood and a delight for the town's small merchants, all of them astounded by her old court styles.

She lived alone in a lane beside the ramparts, in a rather dusty dwelling, for she had no servant. Rising early like people of her age, she would idle about, flitting within her four walls with a feather-duster, lightly brushing a few rare curios caked with dust, scarcely tackling the furniture. At around ten o'clock she would venture out to buy some provisions. It was, to tell the truth, an excuse for bowing and courteous exchanges with the stallholders at the market, for she bought almost nothing to eat, some milk for her cats, and for herself a piece of fruit, a vegetable or two, and at the baker's, half a pastry that would do for a bird.

At the strike of midday she would return to the house, only to leave again at one o'clock, still in her morning clothes, to walk her three white cats on the ramparts, three darling pussies, their necks tied with fat-looped satin bows, and in their ludicrous get-up looking like three little Madame Gorgibuses. She would watch closely to see that Babyface, Tramp, and Blanchette did their business outside, and, this event accomplished, the family would go back into the house where Madame Gorgibus would then perform some skilful pampering.

This would take quite a few hours, but with the lovely sunshine at the end of May and into June, Madame Gorgibus, pompously dressed in old togs and gaudy rags, puffed up in soft-hued cloaks, would shuffle down to the quincunxes, the fashionable promenade where the whole town meets under the most beautiful lime trees in the world, beside the calm blue waters of the Adour River.

The old crone no longer caused a sensation, hardly frightening well-brought-up children: they had seen her time and time again! But there she would meet another original old woman who had also had a reversal of fortune, and who lived on the opposite edge of town, in the neighbourhood of the Capuchin friars.

She was a lady of the nobility, but she no longer received or paid visits, and lived quite secluded from the world. Anyway, she lived too far away and her old legs would have let her down. And then she was somewhat haughty and did not care much for acquainting anyone with her destitution, even her maid Gorgibus who for a long time out of curiosity had besieged the abode. They would meet under the lime trees on the promenade and together spend long hours with the town society round them. Madame de la Livadière knew in minute detail all the stories about these people for at least the past hundred years, and kept trotting them out to her darling friend, all of this in the wonderful setting on the banks of the Adour. What more did these two old dears need? They would see each other again on Sunday at mass, at vespers and at the Benediction of the Blessed Sacrament in their good cathedral. And in the winter months, when the biting cold no longer allowed long rendezvous beside the water on the benches of the promenades, they still found a way to meet.

It was in a chocolate-maker's shop in Bûchettes Street, in the very shadow of the cathedral: a small boutique of white woodwork and tall mirrors streaked with fly specks, a *chocolaterie* of the last century, old-fashioned like its two customers. Apart from the children who would race in to buy a sou's worth of chocolate after mass, no one went there anymore. Chocolate blocks wrapped in tinfoil were sadly turning white at the bottom of the shop windows where sculpted ornaments stood beside sweet wrappers and surprises and *sucres de pomme* whose coloured pictures were growing pale and paler.

And the old lady presiding over the counter, what did she live on? The province has such mysteries. She was a little old woman in a gown of frayed black silk, very clean, with an ever-present lace kerchief covering her curls, silvery curls with yellowing strands, and who, the strange creature, found the means on lovely frosty days to serve Mesdames Gorgibus and de la Livadière, for the sum of thirty centimes a cup, a hot chocolate, my goodness, fragrant, vanillaed and steaming. The ladies would drink it in small sips, pretentious and precious, then compliment the shopkeeper, exchange confidences, and after a few *Darlings*, *My delights* and *My chickens*, each would pay strictly her six sous and depart with a curtsey. How wonderful and touching it was.

And after some exaggerated courtesies they had to go their separate ways: night falls quickly in winter. They would arrange to meet on the first fine day, and Madame de la Livadière, leaning on her ivory-handled cane, would slowly make her way back to her house in the high town, and Madame Gorgibus to her lane near the ramparts, in the Catalan neighbourhood.

And that was it for the day. Once back home, Madame Gorgibus would not go out again. There were preparations for supper, her siesta from five till eight before a few small spoonfuls of soup, then reading from an old almanac, then evening, bed, night. How could such an inoffensive existence attract the hatred of a whole neighbourhood? Her extravagant cloaks, her fashions from another time and her sumptuous rags at first gave people reason to call her a mad old woman; from mad old woman they slipped quickly to wicked old fairy. Leaning on their brooms, the gossips of the town from one doorstep to the next would laugh openly and alert each other to the old mask passing by, her ponytail tied with a ribbon. But Madame Gorgibus had her pride, preferring to shut herself away, and apart from delivery men, she would speak to no one; worse, she would not even open her door to anyone.

What could she have been making in this mysterious dwelling with her three cats? Those three cats, beribboned like brides, made the situation worse: it wasn't natural. What were they doing always sitting beside the cauldron, and what kind of devil's kitchen were they keeping an eye on, then?

The word 'witch' was bandied about, but it was the tamed raven that clinched it.

The old raven, forever standing guard at the corner of the window, sent minds racing. He had a forbidding mien, even threatening, with his huge beak and his round half-asleep eyes; yet, a vigilant soul was evident and his countenance terrified passers-by. Never had a good Christian lived on intimate terms with such a creature; he must have been used for some evil spell and had surely frequented the witches' sabbath. With every passing day, a web of frightful suspicions wound more tightly round Madame Gorgibus.

Unsuspecting, the poor old doll-brained woman continued her humble, habitual existence amid the hostility of everyone. Old, poor, isolated, defenceless, and clueless, sooner or later she would be the victim of some nasty prank; a few boys, always ready for trouble, one day believed it was their right. She was watched and spied upon, and they quickly took advantage of her absence and opened her door, which had been left on the latch, for the poor woman was ever-trusting.

They were not inside long before they seized the three pussycats which were dull from laziness and did not even resist. It was but a minute's work to tie them together securely by their tails with some string and wrap it round the handle of the stew pot. At first the three stunned animals did not move, but as soon as the fire's flame licked their sides they jumped like the damned, and in

a magical leap, yowling, meowing, and screech-
ing across the room, the three animals dragged
the pot right into the middle of the house where
it tipped over. The milk poured out and scalded
them, and cries and meows, whining and rattling
gasps redoubled, and at this the scoundrels could
hardly contain their pleasure; now the raging cats
were eating each other.

However, the oldest two of the gang had not
wasted their time; they had thrown a cover over
the raven, which fought and pecked wildly; but
they had soon wrapped up his head, holding it
between their legs, and, in a flick of the wrist, *click
clack*, they plucked alive the unfortunate throb-
bing bird.

In the blink of an eye Master Raven was stark
naked, most indecent and fantastical with his long
grainy thighs, his stomach the shape of a prow, and
the grey granular skin of his poor shivering body:
a gnome, a vampire, a witches' sabbath beast.

Immobilised by pain, he had taken refuge in
a corner and was not moving except to stupidly
clack his beak. And our rascals fled. Thereupon
Madame Gorgibus came trotting along in her
puce-red silk cape, put her key in the lock and
entered her lodging. What a racket! What a disas-
ter! Deafened by growls and cat cries, she tripped

over a pot around which three animals of the apocalypse were entwined, clasping and devouring each other, their fur bristling and sticky. One of them clawed her hand in a long scratch, another sank his teeth into her calf, and while in her frenzy she tried calling for help, her throat would produce not even one cry, while a nightmarish bird, a ghostly animal, livid, obscene, with two wings of grey flesh, rushed at her with his beak wide open, hopping up and down, trying to climb her skirts. Fortunately, Madame Gorgibus could get back to her door and she ran screaming through the night, and what little sanity she had was dimmed by the adventure.

Madame Gorgibus went mad. She finished her days in the asylum.

III

Gudule the Maid

Madame de Lautréamont lived in the most beautiful house in town. It was the former Office of the Receiver General, built under Louis XV (none less!). Its high windows, adorned with emblems and shells, were admired by everyone who passed through the large square on market days. The great dwelling was flanked by two wings set at right angles and joined by a wide gate, forming the courtyard of honour, and behind the main building was the most beautiful garden in the world. From terrace to terrace it descended down to the ramparts and dominated thirty leagues of countryside, and, in the most beautiful Louis XV layout, it sheltered in its groves some licentious statues, all of them variously tormented by Laughter and Love.

The apartments of the house were lined with sculpted panels with a most charming effect, and were decorated with pillars and mirrors. Even the parquetry of the entire ground floor, curiously inlaid with wood from the West Indies, shone like a mirror. Madame de Lautréamont lived only in the principal part; she had rented the wings to solid tenants and made for herself a nice private income. There was no one who wouldn't want to live in the Lautréamont mansion; it was a never-ending subject of conversation around town.

Now, this Madame de Lautréamont was born with a silver spoon in her mouth, and had always had every opportunity: a husband built like Hercules and entirely subject to her will, who let her be dressed by a renowned tailor in Paris; two children whom she had set up in life, the daughter married to a Royal Prosecutor, and the son already captain of the artillery, or was about to be; the most beautiful home in the region; and a state of health which kept her still fresh, and, oh my, desirable at more than forty-five years of age. To maintain this princely residence and her almost indecent health, she had a domestic like they don't make anymore, a superior individual, the rare pearl of all servants. Every form of devotion, attention, and honesty was embodied in Gudule the maid.

Because of this wonderful girl, Madame de Lautréamont managed to keep her huge house with three servants, a gardener, a valet, and a cook on an income of just sixty thousand pounds. It was unquestionably the best-kept residence in town: not a speck of dust on the marble console tables; parquet floors dangerous for being so well polished; old mirrors clearer than the water in the fountains; and everywhere, in all the apartments, an order, a symmetry. And people spoke of the old building of the Receiver General as though it were the prime household of the province, saying, with what became henceforth the accepted way of designating a well-kept dwelling: 'You'd think we were in the Lautréamonts' house.'

The soul of this astonishing residence happened to be the good old spinster with small naïve blue eyes and cheeks still fresh, who, from morning to night, feather-duster or broom in hand, serious, silent, and active, never stopped beating, brushing, dusting, and making things shine and gleam, the declared enemy of every atom of dust. The other servants feared her a little: it was a terrible thing to be supervised by Gudule the maid. She was wholly devoted to the interests of her masters, and nothing escaped her little blue eye. What's more, she was always in the house, for the old girl only went out to attend mass on celebration days and Sundays, and in truth she was hardly devout and not at all strict about the six o'clock mass, that excuse all the old servant women used for a daily outing.

In town they never stopped singing the praises of this model housekeeper, and Madame de Lautréamont was greatly envied for her servant. A few souls wanting in delicacy were unscrupulous enough to try to pinch her. They made Gudule lucrative offers, for vanity was a part of it, and, in society, bets were even opened to remove the poor girl from her mistress; but it was a waste of time. Gudule, with the loyalty of another age, turned a deaf ear to every proposition, and the insolent happiness of Madame de Lautréamont continued until the day when the old servant, worn out, exhausted from work, died like a lamp without oil in her cold little attic under the roof, where Madame de Lautréamont, it must be said to her credit, remained three days.

Gudule the maid had the joy of dying with her dear mistress at her bedside. The Lautréamonts had a suitable burial for their servant. Monsieur de Lautréamont conducted the mourning. Gudule had her concession in the cemetery, fresh flowers on her grave for at least eight days, then they really needed to replace her.

Replace her, no, for that would be impossible, but at least they could bring into the mansion a woman to do her job. House mistresses can be found, and after a few unhappy trials Madame de Lautréamont believed she could finally congratulate herself for having laid hands on a woman she could trust, a woman of great integrity.

Mademoiselle Agatha reigned henceforth in the old Receiver's offices. She was a rather plump woman, her bosom projecting bastion-like, and she rushed about gesticulating, appalled at every turn, a bunch of keys on her belt, an apron of shot silk on her waist, and airs of Madame Braggart; her service was not exactly silent. From morning to night there was nothing but whining after the other servants, and the old residence, so calm and so quiet in Gudule's time, was now deafened by it all. But Mademoiselle Agatha knew how to make herself look good, and that was the secret. All it took was daily reports on the antechamber and the kitchen, self-interested disputes with the cook, and in the end Madame de Lautréamont was taken in by all these displays of noisy devotion.

Oh! This was no longer Gudule's service, invisible and silent, like housework done by a shadow, that discreet and almost frightened attention that accompanies a secret devotion, a vigilance every second of the day, the meticulous ways of a spinster who adored her masters' home, the devotee's worship of her parish and all the domestic fervour that was in the Lautréamonts' home in earlier times, like perfume for the altar.

There were now specks of dust on the marble of the console tables, the old mirrors in the drawing-rooms no longer imitated the clear water of the fountains any more than the parquet floors imitated the mirrors. But habit is such a force and Gudule had created such a legend that the old Receiver General's mansion was still cited whenever discussions arose about the best-kept house in the region.

Now, some six months later (it was mid-November and Gudule had passed away in March), one night Madame de Lautréamont abruptly woke Monsieur de Lautréamont, and in a voice somewhat changed, without even lighting the candle, she said:

'Hector, that's odd! Listen! It sounds like Gudule's broom sweeping.'

Monsieur de Lautréamont, in a very bad mood as a man still half asleep, grumbled and told her she was mad. But Madame de Lautréamont, with great emotion, was shaking so violently that this model husband made an effort to wake up properly and listen closely to his wife's ravings.

'I tell you, someone is there,' she continued, 'there, on the upstairs landing, at our bedroom door. I can hear footsteps, but why this sound of sweeping? See! It's further away now, there's sweeping at the end of the hall, and I tell you it's her way of sweeping. Just you think about it; I know her.'

Madame de Lautréamont dared not even say the name again, and Monsieur de Lautréamont, in his understanding, said:

'The truth is, that girl is running through your head! Your wakefulness is but a dream, my dear, I'm certain there's nothing there. The air is so still that we can't even hear a leaf rustling. It's your dinner sitting on your stomach. Would you like me to make you a cup of tea?'

But Madame de Lautréamont, trembling all over, had shot off the end of the bed like a spring and was running barefoot across the room toward the door. She opened it, peeked out, and with a ghastly shriek shut it again. Monsieur de Lautréamont leapt to her side, understanding nothing of this burst of madness, and took his almost senseless wife to a large wing chair into which she dropped, unable to breathe for a time. Finally her voice returned, and in the now illuminated bedroom, she said:

'It's her, I saw her just as I can see you. She was there, sweeping and scrubbing the parquetry in our hall, in the homespun dress that you knew her by, in the bonnet she wore when alive, but so white, so deathly pale! Oh! It's like something from the cemetery! We will have to have some masses said for her, my love.'

Monsieur de Lautréamont calmed his wife as best he could, yet he remained worried and pensive, for they were to see things that were even more mysterious.

The following night, Madame de Lautréamont's hallucination returned. Shivering, her teeth clenched in terror, she could now hear the deceased servant polishing and scrubbing the large deserted landing, bustling about, her feet shod with brushes. Could fear be contagious? The large house was sleeping, and this time, in the silence, Monsieur de Lautréamont could hear it, and despite his wife clutching his arm in horror he went boldly to the door, opened it, and looked out.

Every hair on his damp flesh stood up: the disintegrating figure of the dead servant was shuffling and wriggling, a funereal marionette in the middle of the empty hall. She was bathed in a moonbeam shining through a window over the staircase, and in the luminous blue ray the dead woman went back and forth, brushing and scrubbing in feverish agitation. It was like the work of a condemned woman, and as she passed Monsieur de Lautréamont he distinctly saw drops of sweat on her already smooth skull. He quickly shut the door, terrified and convinced.

'You're right,' he said simply as he turned to his wife, 'we will have to have a few masses said for that girl.'

Ten masses were said for the defunct, ten low masses which Monsieur and Madame de Lautréamont and their whole household attended, and Gudule the maid returned no more to do the work of Mademoiselle Agatha on clear November nights.

IV

Queen Maritorne

When I have told the story of the apparition of Queen Maritorne who hung heavily over my whole childhood like a dark nightmare, I will have ended the series of my little tales, finished the suite of these bland stories with their dated and antiquated odour with which Norine charmed my early years and which even now still bring to mind images of a part of the provinces which today has disappeared, a part of society quite forgotten, and with it the indefinable charm that accompanied certain arbours and lime tree walks at the end of October: a faded, piquant smell of mouldering cemetery earth, odours of ether and dead leaves.

Queen Maritorne was the terror of greedy thieving children: she reigned from the attic, where lines of pears and apples ripened, to the vat from which the wine was drawn; she was also the punishment for drunks, and without warning would leap out of the cask fraudulently tapped by the indiscreet valet. No one had ever seen her but they knew she was present and vigilant everywhere. She was in the jam jar that sly children drooled over, as she was in the half-light of kitchen pantries; the pot-bellied chest of drawers, into which grannies crammed their tins of marzipan and boxes full of bergamot orange berlingots, was equally protected by her, and whoever took the risk of opening the sweets cupboard might very well have found Queen Maritorne lying stretched out in a drawer.

She held all rights over the gluttonous child who made himself sick at the table, and in the folds of her gown she carried terrifying indigestion; to the guilty she distributed fevers and colics like manna; and every rebellious stomach was hers. She was also resident in kitchens, lying in ambush behind the preserving pans and enormous copper saucepans where in autumn the venison stew simmered; she haunted dark cellars, and orchards heavy with the scent of medlars, and the obstructive shadow of large piles of vegetables from the sculleries.

Such as she was, indistinct and vague in everyone's imagination, her obese and paunchy figure weighed uncomfortably on the conscience and stomach of servants and rascally children.

And so, little Wilhem was greatly terrified when, carried away from the table for having stuffed himself like a pig on plum tart and cream-puffs, he found he was lying in his little bed, in his dark and lonely bedroom, with the beginning of a stomach-ache, alone in the large room where he slept with his nanny, all alone on the third floor of this huge five-storey house while everyone was still downstairs at dinner.

His nanny, eager to return to the other servants, had left him without light, and through the high window over which she had forgotten to close the curtains the moonlight shone and spread an immense white sheet over the floor, freezing the uncertain contours of objects into weird poses.

And suddenly all through the haunted room unfamiliar profiles grimaced: at first it was the faded pastel drawing of the grandfather beneath the glass of its picture frame. He was straight as a monstrance, his muslin cravat tied high about the neck, a morning coat the colour of deerskin open over a frilled shirt, and he bore the austere, clean-shaven face of a magistrate of old. All of a sudden his brows knit together and a flash of justifiable indignation lit up his pupils; the unfortunate little Wilhem's stomach churned, and, terrified, he quickly turned his eyes away. But his gaze fell on an armchair where a pile of ambiguous clothes lay slumping in the shadows. Slowly, the flaccid trouser legs came to life and two surprising feet popped out; and while the torso was rising in a sudden flight of the jacket, two nervous little arms wrapped themselves tightly against a scrawny chest and a sinister little old man's head sniggered in the silence. What a grin! The thirty-two keys of the harpsichord appeared all white in the nutcracker face of the strange little being.

But it was nothing more than an apparition. The bedroom had again returned to the shadows and when Wilhem, who had hidden his head under the sheets, ventured a frightened peek out of the bedcovers, he no longer saw anything abnormal; everything had resumed its usual place, the objects shrouded in twilight were as though faded into the night, and he was hardly even anxious about his water jug sitting on the chest of drawers, strangely crouching in the middle of the washbowl like an enormous white toad.

And little Wilhem began to breathe again, but his peace of mind did not last long. He quickly pricked his ear at an unusual sound. On the stairs now there were footsteps, footsteps, and more footsteps, like the stamping of an army on the march. A crowd was hurrying up the steps; he heard them jostle each other on the second-floor landing, then mount the staircase to the third floor. They were surely coming to his bedroom.

And with a great flood of light his door burst open. He couldn't even scream. All the kitchen pots and pans were there, stumbling over the threshold; they were gleaming copper sauce-pans filled to the brim with rice and bread soup, huge preserving pans waddling along heavily on three improvised legs, and Savoie biscuit moulds, and big kettles with evil faces, obviously ill-intentioned, and teapots with metallic glints, and hostile-looking coffeepots with long insidious spouts. All these things were swarming, colliding, and moving silently into the middle of the room; it was like a creeping of ghostly objects over the floor. They surrounded his bed, and, like a silent tide, slowly rose and ebbed and rose again along his bed covers.

Bathed in sweat, his eyes wide with horror, the child could not say a word: the invasion was quite terrifying. The bedroom was full of all these dream-like copper utensils and pewter-ware, and at the door still more were coming. And now, joining the large forbidding kettles and menacing coffee-pots, there were sausages with legs, hams with gnome faces, and ghostly chickens flying around the bedroom, all on a spit, all roasted.

Jugged hare heads were lifting saucepan lids; cheeping lark beaks were trying to escape from another pan; purees of beans and peas were bubbling and popping in brown earthenware dishes; a goose barded with lard was dancing and quacking, its rump fully trussed, ready for the spit; and some pigeons, escaped from the steamer, formed a cortège of boiled meat processing toward a fricassee of rabbit in wine. It was something frightful, and in this fantastic culinary ceremony the distraught Wilhem recognised Queen Maritorne.

She was there, gigantic, impassive, armoured in red copper and clumping along in her heavy crinoline dress, her form imprisoned in a soup tureen. What could be seen of her skin was sautéed and browned like the stomach of a turkey roasted a long time in the kitchen fire, and for hands she had two enormous chicken feet. She was a horrible creature, bald and hairless, and on her skull she had the fanned tail of a peacock trimmed and dressed for the table. A collar of saveloys played across the faïence of her chest, and two monstrous chitterlings hung from her belt by way of a ceremonial pendant. In one hand she held a bouquet of leeks, onions, and carrots, and, as the true queen of the stew pot, she brandished with the other hand a huge ladle and relentlessly dipped into the purees, the roux, the sauces, and the bread soups, menacing the child's terror with them. But the thing he could not bear was the eye of a ghostly doll, a mechanical eye, enamel and lifeless, staring at him. He managed a loud scream ... and awoke this time to the light of a lamp and a candle; his mother, his sisters, and his nanny were fussing around him. He awoke sheepish, his face downcast: little Wilhem had had an accident in his bed.

Useless Virtue

In my grandmother's house, the very one where I spent my holidays, a Louis XIII house with a high roof, its dormer windows always closed, there was across the entire length of the dwelling an immense attic. Old things from centuries past were piled up under the dust; asleep and bathing in a soft glow, brushed by light slipping between the tiles, a pile of extraordinary things made us dream, especially me, a small boy already curious and anxious, my imagination always aroused, and precociously excitable. Any excuse was good for sneaking away from the linen room where Norine was busy sewing and keeping an eye on our games. I would climb the stairs four at a time, my heart aching deliciously. I would stop, out of breath, at the door of this coveted attic, fearing I would find it closed and dreading no less it would be open. I always hesitated before entering; it was for me a place of mystery, a sort of strangely populated retreat. Its inhabitants were tall armoires filled with books, and in those books there were pictures; and then there was an old secretaire with drawers and a writing tablet bound with green morocco stained with ink, and a large clock with figures that were supposed to appear, but the clock didn't work anymore; there was also a map of the world painted with bluish continents, an old paint box and other things like it that I gazed at in ecstasy for a long time, hardly daring to touch them. And I loved to stay there for hours and hours, because there I felt far away from everything, in an atmosphere supernatural and bizarre, in a kind of light that was like no other, transparent and green, as at the bottom of the sea. In this silence, amid all these old things fallen into neglect, antiquated, forgotten, there was an undulating and murky atmosphere of watery abysses. Then there were all those books, most of them in German which I didn't understand, but I would look at the pictures and there were such a lot of pictures! Of all of them, one volume appealed to me; it was a book of stories. The title, I can't remember; on the first page there was a plate depicting Death with an hourglass and a young girl, it was hideous; then there were others with churches, palaces, streets, and large vessels that go on the sea; I read all the stories in that book but I remember none; still, I would know them if I heard them: a child's brain is made of wax that accepts only those sensations that are pressed into it. But when I think of that attic, I immediately see a blue-green vision with seaweed moving through it, and shimmering reflections, and large collapsed things: they are yardarms, masts and ships like cathedrals, spectres of flotsam from bygone days, ghosts from very old shipwrecks, and from all these phantoms I can truly produce only one story, a vague story about a symbol, fleeting and sad, that escaped me at the time. Did I read this story as it was, or is it rather the confusion of several other stories gathered haphazardly and inconsistently and badly digested by my young imagination?

Such as it is, murky, trembling, and diffuse, it still pleases me like a reflection remaining in a mirror clouded by verdigris: so I will call it *Story from my Attic*, for that is its real title, rather than this paraphrase of its symbolic text: *Useless Virtue*.

For three long days he had been riding along the dunes where pale thistles flowered. Not one sail whitened the horizon: from dawn till dusk, there was the monotone expanse of a calm sea, an unruffled sea the colour of slate beneath the dismal glare of a white sky. Sometimes his horse would suddenly skid to a halt and neigh at the sea; and in a silken startling of wings some gulls disturbed from a hole in the cliff would whirl high up in the air, then disappear, and the red sand would ripple with their shadow.

And the young man would not even lift his head. With his brow furrowed beneath the outstretched eagle wings on his helmet, he was making his way, deep in thought, along the foot of the cliff, a high wall of schist running for leagues beside the sad sea. Some dried grasses of a mauve hue hung like hair halfway up the side of the rock, dead hair, inhabited only by a few rare sea birds.

In the evenings the cliffs turned pink, even the dunes were set alight by the fire of the sunset, and the young man would dismount and leave his horse to graze the blue thistles of the sands and seek to stave off his own thirst, his hunger too, by biting the salty flesh from a few shells. And then, beneath the rising moon, he would continue on his way.

In the cloister where he had been raised under the command of the queen, his mother, he had taken a vow to find, dead or alive, the fair-haired knight to whom he owed his birth: Bertram was the fruit of a sin. The bastard child of the Queen of Aquitaine's fornication had been nurtured and nourished by her, even as an adulterous princess, as the idea of vengeance: she had sworn that the son of her lust would be made to find the unfaithful lover who had abandoned her. The young prince had grown up in a convent of Barnabites; the queen had taken charge of his education, invisible, masked, unknown to this son whom she destined to a tragic end. The monks had raised the child harshly in the hatred of the love of women and of all that laughs and flowers under the sun. Fasting and prayer had hardened the soul of this son of a queen, who wore a hair shirt under his damascened armour and a triple cord of hemp tied round his waist. And then, one fine morning, bewitched by a magic potion, the palms of his hands and soles of his feet rubbed with the blood of a shewolf, the young avenger was released into the countryside.

'You will recognise the man who made your childhood bleak and vexed by the triple emerald glowing in its setting on the crest of his helmet. Whether his hair be snow white or golden, strike and kill, and you will have avenged your humiliated life, your mother, your race, and your God.'

The fateful words were pronounced in a dream voice, in the very chapel of the convent where he had spent the eve of this battle. A form concealed in the shadows had dictated the judgment, and the next day at dawn Bertram had gone into the country, gloved, breast-plated, masked in nielloed silver from his helmet's crest to the star of his spurs, and above his morion was the tawny gold double flash of an enormous eagle beating its wings.

Up in the convent's bell tower, a woman had long been watching him in the flush of the burgeoning day. When the silhouette of the young adventurer had vanished into the distant heather, the queen had gone and prostrated herself before the high altar where nightfall found her still muttering and praying.

And now as he was riding beneath moonlight that silvered the calm sea, the memory of strange encounters oppressed the young warrior.

At first it had been, on the third evening after his departure from the cloister, a vision of three young girls at the edge of the wood, the three daughters of the old lord as they had called themselves when greeting him familiarly by his name.

Sitting at the entrance of the forest, they had stood up at the sight of him and tried to garland his palfrey's bridle with flowers. They were inviting and cheerful with hoods of anemones over their swinging braids and they seemed naked under their new tunics of leaf-patterned silk. Standing in the dew, the group had surrounded him like a circle of nimble dancers, and with their bearing, the caress of their eyes and voices, and their cool, supple arms, they had tried to keep him there. But he had brutally driven his horse onward at the risk of knocking them over—prairie elves have a habit of appearing to travellers like this in the evening—and he had gone full tilt beneath the boughs, wild and deliberately deaf to their appeal.

He had ridden for two nights and two days in the oak forest, and then the high shady treetops had given way to broad clearings, and the clearings to mournful plains traversed by screens of aspen. Ponds sparkled among the tall grasses, and mists drifted night and day, weaving what seemed to be shrouds around equivocal willow trunks. Then he had entered a region of peat bogs and pale marshes where blackish soil yielded underfoot; and one moonless night as he rode alongside one of these grim swamps, his palfrey suddenly reared up under him and Bertram looked up and saw, standing on the leaden water, a supernatural, livid nude.

It was a woman's body of an alarming pallor, but her eyes and her smile were filled with a strange ecstasy. She had emerged like a will-o'-the-wisp above a clump of water lilies, smiling drunkenly, as though contorted in a spasm, her breasts rearing up, her mouth open, a small silver mirror in her hand.

A freak moon had sprung up in the same moment behind the willow plantation, and the woman, blessed in death and glinting like mother-of-pearl, blocked the young man's passage, offering him both her bluish mouth and the mirror's image. An old willow, its branches lopped, had suddenly reflected in the pond as the figure of a faun, and when the young warrior had pushed away the wanton corpse in horror, an enormous frog jumped from the grass and dived with a dull thud into the deathly pale water.

And Bertram, walking along the sands, thought about all these magic spells, all these traps and illusions. What did they want from him, these masks from the shadows, these wandering figures of the night, and what was the symbol of all these temptations?

And he became aware that a silent galley, of

which he had perceived neither a rustling of sails nor a beating of oars, was bordering the shore at the same time as he. The tall masts, the rigging and yards were transparent against the darkness, and it looked like a dream ship, for it did not so much cleave through the waves as glide over the water, and everything on board seemed to be sleeping a deep sleep. Not one sailor on the bridge. Abandoned vessel, or ghost ship? The waves did not even lap about its sides, and the ashen galley proceeded mysteriously side by side with him, and Bertram would have believed he had been tricked by another vision if he had not discerned, leaning on the prow, a motionless old man, the pilot no doubt, his fingers tormenting a lyre, but an enchanted lyre, for the chords he touched made no sound.

And with daylight Bertram found himself in a region of undulations and small hills broken by quickset hedges and apple orchards: the ghost ship, the pink sandy shore and the high cliff had vanished, and the young adventurer, starting to think nothing could surprise him, spurred his horse on across the pastures and hawthorn hedges of this orchard country. Here was the most profound solitude; he could sense the closeness of the sea by the hue of the sky swept

free of clouds, and the apple trees twisted by the wind, and he had already been riding for five long hours on a type of sunken path when a beautiful woman appeared to him. She was wearing brocade wrought with aspen leaves, and slender and straight as a lily she was riding bareback on a unicorn, an elegant and fabulous dream beast, its hair gleaming like metal. The lady on the unicorn was wearing on her black hair a gold helmet surmounted by a small crown and, like a knight, she held a lance couched at the ready.

She blocked the young sire's passage, and while threatening him with her lance, she gave the lie to her evil intention with a smile, showing Bertram an enormous red rose bleeding at her waist. But he had nothing but murder on his mind. With the back of his sword he pushed aside the beautiful warrior's fine steel lance and ignored her.

As he passed by, the beautiful lady whipped his face with the rose from her gorget, but it was a dry rose, its petals falling, and the young man, having turned round in surprise, saw nothing but an old woman galloping away on a donkey. 'Yet another of the Devil's traps!' he thought to himself, and he continued along the road, a little sadder, a little more weary.

Finally he arrived at a sort of inn. A pine

branch shaded the door and three beautiful girls were standing before the threshold. Their breasts free in short homespun gowns, bareheaded and barefoot, they were laughing heartily in the crepuscular heat: one was spinning at the distaff; another, leaning over a stone trough, was retting hemp; and the third, at sight of the young man, dashed back into the inn but emerged again with a jug of wine. She offered Bertram a drink and the other two urged him to dismount.

They smelled of sweat, of bread and lavender, but Bertram pushed them away. With peals of laughter they went back inside, closed the door of the inn, and the young man remained alone on the high road.

Now, his mount had gone over to the trough to drink and, as the palfrey was quenching its thirst, Bertram, who had leaned forward, cried out.

The royal adventurer had just appeared to himself, the depths of the trough had become a mirror, and it was the face of an old man that smiled at him, the face of an old warrior with a long grey beard, his gaze weary and sad, his smile forgiving, a wan face from the past girt by a golden helmet where three emeralds glistened like tears, and Bertram recognised the man whom he had to strike down. It was himself, then, whom he had to kill by striking his image, and, his heart heavy with the deepest sorrow, Bertram understood that he had grown old. This grey hair was his, and these lifeless eyes, alas, had become his eyes, and he understood, too late, that he had pursued an impossible adventure. Life should be lived without scorning love, lust, pleasure, or even the passing opportunity, and he had let himself be deluded by a deceptive mirage, like the pilot of the silent ship ... And now it was no use thinking of turning back ... for every hour flees, and cannot be redeemed.

Marjolaine

This story is an old song from my childhood; I've tried to recall its rhythm and rhyme as best I can. I think I can still hear the plaintive voices of the servants who sang it, not at my grandmother's, but in my parents' home. Ah, that was a long time ago, in the small coastal town where I spent my earliest years. They would sing it on Christmas Eve while awaiting midnight mass, and it was in the kitchen of my parental home that the song first filled me with wonder as a child captivated by legends, always escaping from the drawing-room to go and curl up in the skirts of the servant girls and listen to them turn their hopes and fears into poetry with vague popular refrains.

Now, among all this fanciful nonsense, I loved with a very special affection the story of a beautiful girl who was carried away, her skirts upside down, beneath the clouds frozen by the terrible wind from the north-west, the *Noroué*, which even during the storytelling we could hear groaning down there below the cliffs.

On the North Bridge they were dancing,
a strong cold wind was blowing,
and it carried away Marjolaine.

Marjolaine, in her skirt of fustian
and her woollen stockings.
Clouds brushed by as she soared on high,

And far from the town,
the poor girl flew round
circling and dashing through the sky.

As she swirled,
'Jesus and Mary,' she called,
'since toward death I drift,

When stunned from my fall swift,
let me come as you find me
into your heaven gold and starry.'

And beneath icy skies and bitter
came for her prayer an answer
on the belfry of Saint Evremond's.

Marjolaine, a soul distraught,
was abruptly suspended, caught
by a hole in her underskirt.

On this night, rainy and cold,
the silent gargoyle, suddenly bold,
began to speak in words overt:

'The fustian is flimsy, your time is near.
Alas! Think on this, do you hear
the Devil jeering?'

And in the raging autumn wind
the frightened shivering beauty was pinned,
and from above the void was peering.

She counted, in the dusky night,
roofs turning blue in the moonlight,
and in the deserted church square, the saints.

And the Devil was already laughing
as a perfume arose, emanating
from benzoin, nard and incense.

And holding branches of palm,
up into space and under skies calm
ascended some grand old men;

Grand old men, white-robed,
balding heads hanging drooped
over copes of heavy brocade, and then

There were virgins parading
in gowns cascading
with stars and scattered lilies,

Their foreheads wreathed in aureoles.
Long archangels in stoles
formed a cortège, and with pure eyes

Of sombre blue and souls distinct,
in great flaming streaks they flew linked,
crisscrossing the brumous moon and the night skies.

With ghosts of holy virgins did they rise,
and with the elect, and angels,
and psalms and noëls,

In ceremony they led
Marjolaine, who was dead,
into Jesus' paradise.

I imagined this Marjolaine to be similar in every way to the beautiful, robust Norman women who served in my mother's house; they wore the same costume as in the song—woollen stockings and fustian skirts—and in my precocious imagination it was my nanny, Héloïse, who took care of me, and whom I seemed to see spinning like a top above the jetties streaming with sea-foam, a long, long way from the famous North Bridge of the ballad, which I would confuse with both the Avignon Bridge and the footbridge of the port jetty just in front of our house.

It was on the belfry of Saint Etienne's, our parish church, that I suspended her by the hole in her underskirt; but strangely it was on the towers of Saint Ouen's, bristling with grimacing figures, serpents with dragon heads, dragons with lion heads, and winged frogs, that I placed the deathly dialogue of gargoyles.

> On this night, rainy and cold,
> the silent gargoyle, suddenly bold,
> began to speak in words overt:

Oh! This lapidary discourse of the bewitched gargoyle bathed in bright silvery moonlight, it gave me a delicious thrill of terror!

I saw the granite beast shoot its blind sculpted eyeballs from their sockets; it had slightly straightened its long neck, scaly as a cuirass; some folds in the immutably hardened stone seemed to quiver under its stomach, and glimmers of moonlight flowed like slaver between its lizard jaws.

I had seen and noted this heraldic monster in my childish mind when I went up the towers of Saint Ouen's on a long-ago trip to Rouen, and through a strange association of memories it was the roofs, the belfries, the whole panorama of the old Norman town that I imagined Marjolaine was frantically looking down over as she hung on the belfry of Saint Evremond's.

And in the raging autumn wind
the frightened shivering beauty was pinned,
and from above the void was peering.

She counted, in the dusky night,
roofs turning blue in the moonlight,
and in the deserted church square, the saints.

A woman's thigh squeezed above the knee by a blue garter also haunted my memory. I still shared my nanny's bedroom and it often happened that I could watch this honourable girl undress in moments when she was feeling a little less embarrassed, believing I was asleep. This glimpsed patch of skin obsessed me and made me blush; it was Héloïse's robust nudity that I ascribed to Marjolaine, suspended shivering above the winter-besieged roofs.

The psalms and music rising up in the night around the dying girl were for me the *adeste fideles*, the hymn I would hear at the coming mass. The stained-glass windows of the church had acquainted me with the patriarchs with long flowing beards and the saintly women of the liberating cortège in long leaf-patterned robes; the choir children personified for me the youthful procession of angels; and as I was leaving midnight mass, still mellow from the hymns and incense, I would stop just a few steps from the porch and look up to see if the ascending bishops and virgins of the legend were spiralling round Saint Etienne's belfry.

But only the snow and moonlight haunted the old Romanesque tower where no gargoyle was keeping watch. I had been daydreaming, lulled by the spinning-wheel hum of this old Flemish tale, which in my mind had become a pious tale for Christmas.

About a Portrait

The one I will tell you now is more of a true story than a tale; I have partly lived it but I have dreamed it more, and so it is still a tale. Reality prepares the canvas and imagination embroiders it, and the reader will forgive me for cheating with this impression half-lived, half-dreamed; it is the last of this little book and it closes a series of unremarkable, old-fashioned stories with the deepest and most melancholy impression of a childhood that was all melancholy and dreams.

Among the homes where my grandparents would take me on visits, there is one whose memory, enveloped in fondness and faded into half-tints, has left the impression of a caress. Yet it was a rather cold house of an old maid who was somewhat ridiculous, an old noble spinster with a large nose daubed with tobacco, and beneath the ribbons flying from her bonnet she had the look of an old president rather than the canoness d'Estournelle.

Mademoiselle Olympe d'Estournelle lived at the corner of Saint Fursy Place and Clockmakers Street, in a squat old house like a Louis XV chest of drawers, its whole first floor overhanging some small beams sculpted with faces and grimacing dwarves. Between the windows, slender statues of bishops and saints, partly decapitated, were praying with their hands together. This residence, which had had the honour of accommodating Louis XI in the year … at the time of his passage to Montfort, a few days before the famous interview in Péronne with the Duke of Burgundy, was for three centuries the town house of the d'Estournelle family. The old spinster, whose unexceptional face today summons me as a mature man as much as it intrigued me in the past as a small boy, lived there alone, the last daughter of her family, amid a staff of servants from another time, in a setting of outdated and touching luxury.

Tall, bony, angular, and dry, in stiff crackling dresses of golden brown fabrics, with the air of an old goat—as she herself would say, ironically aware of her ugliness—fundamentally good and of a generosity proverbial among the destitute, but quite the free-thinker like many women brought up during the Revolution, and, knowing she was blessed, giving in her turn blessings to the poor, Mademoiselle d'Estournelle had the most open salon in Montfort. Her house was the centre and meeting place of all society, and every Friday during Lent she gave light dinners, the menus of which, cleverly and carefully put together, were mentioned as far away as the home of the Monsignor of Amiens.

This old spinster, scorned by love—or at least, warned by her mirror, she'd had a wise mistrust of love—unlike many disappointed sour old birds, adored young people and children; at every opportunity she gave her nephews and grand-cousins sorbets, told them stories and sang them songs. Each one of her delicious dinners, served in solid silverware, was followed by improvised dances: young people need to enjoy themselves. During Carnaval, the most beautiful balls were held in her home, the craziest masquerades were in her home; on those evenings the lovely old lady handed her house over to her guests. The secular armoires from the upper bedrooms, dead grannies' jewellery cabinets, and the entire wardrobe of the former Countesses d'Estournelle were pillaged. And down the grand staircase with its oak balusters and wide half-landings there was a stampede of slim waspish waists in the bodices of the time, pretty girls in hoop petticoats, their dance partners in vests floriated in old pastels, all the d'Estournelles' cast-offs, not seen these days, on the backs of the grand-nephews and grand-nieces who would be in fits of laughter and delighted to be dressed like the ancestors of the salon.

But these were the capers of the oldest ones in the gang; and for me—a small boy still too young to take part in the evening's amusements and already too old to be invited to the little girls' tea parties—were reserved long afternoons chatting with the old cousin in her large bedroom on the first floor. It was quite an exceptional favour; I was allowed to browse the collections of *La Mode*, an album of prints, already yellowing, depicting the voluminous coiffures and extravagant dresses of the last years of Louis XVI.

Oh! This fashion collection and these illustrations where the dominant colours were canary yellow, and the purplish-brown hue of *flea in milk fever* and a shade of pink called *bright shepherdess*!

I would see beautiful ladies, their bosom exposed, a sky-high coiffure above a dress in the Greek antique style, or even in a *hussar* style short jacket and a *King of Prussia* hat, who answered to the lovely names of Zémire and Thémidore, two gallant pseudonyms whose personalities my old cousin sometimes revealed to me. And it was the former court that she would then evoke with a word and a gesture: Zémire was the Duchess de Polignac,[2] that ungrateful little woman; Thémidore, that charming Madame de Coislin.[3]

There was also the glass cabinet of old Dresden china statuettes from which was taken out, oh, very rarely, the monkey orchestra. Twenty beribboned baboons, pink and green figurines, at least finger height, would play all the instruments; one on the violin, one on the bassoon, one on the viola d'amore, one on the oboe, one on the flute and even on the viola da gamba, one on the theorbo and, if I remember rightly, one on the psaltery, in absolutely hilarious and surprisingly diverse poses.

---

2. The Duchess de Polignac was the favourite of Marie Antoinette.

3. Madame de Coislin had an affair with Louis XV, and was therefore a rival of Madame de Pompadour.

My cousin, looking most serious, claimed that all these baboons and monkeys were most likely playing a tune by Monsieur de Lully,[4] that she saw it in their solemn, enamoured faces, that His Majesty King Louis was going to appear in the mirror, that this was obvious and no one could be mistaken about it.

Lastly, there was the armoire of cakes and pralines and cashew pastilles. It was sitting right in the corner near the chimney and Mademoiselle d'Estournelle always carried its key hanging on the chain on her belt. This key chain was yet another curiosity. Jiggling and jingling on it were firstly a watch in blue enamel, then a medallion of sharkskin containing some kind of painting, then another in crystal with a lock of hair, a small Dresden china bottle of perfume, a pair of silver-gilt scissors, and thrown on at the end, the key to the cellar, as enormous and menacing as the key to the town gates.

Mademoiselle d'Estournelle's bedroom! I spent such happy days there in my childhood, the best of my life perhaps, beside this old spinster, her heart considerate and tender, very tender despite

---

4. Monsieur de Lully wrote music known for its liveliness and deep emotional character.

her capricious gruffness and cheeriness, yes, the lovely cosy hours in this massive, high-ceilinged room of white woodwork from last century. The windows looked onto the rampart, and winter and summer there was the mournful gleam of the Sorgue swamps, slate grey in winter when the river was frozen, the colour of tin under the white skies of summer, and in mid-autumn toward the end of October when the boatmen of Avrain-court and Boin came to cut the reeds, there was yet another kind of melancholy in the fog-cloaked atmosphere: the silky softened rustling of all the freshly cut green stalks lying on the water.

And connected in my memory to this sound of reed-cutting, I don't know why, is the memory of a portrait, a portrait of a man, a painting which barely caught my eye, being silhouetted against the daylight, a darkened figure, seldom noticed in my childhood; but what's strange is that its features have become much clearer as I go through life.

I remember this haunting portrait hung between two windows, above a spinet in old Martin's varnish where some roses and carnations in a wreath were flaking away. A secretaire in white cedar occupied the space between the other windows, and in my childhood it was the secretaire that especially interested me, because of an enormous fishbowl filled with water from Notre-Dame de Liesse sitting on its marble top.

Oh! This bowl of miraculous water with all those relics in blown glass, miniature doves, ladders of the Passion and saintly Lilliputian women going up and down like bubbles in a ceaseless madness of movement, what a place it held then in my life as a child curious about everything and about everything amazed! It was the goldfish bowl of the ideal: vitrified goldfish, ethereal, frozen, spiritualised. So in those days the portrait left me quite cold, the portrait which now haunts me and that I would very much like to rediscover.

What happened to it? Which junk shop is it lying around in, its frame without gilding and, even in my time, its canvas flaking; which junk shop is it in, or which museum? It was a man's portrait, a very young man, in Louis XIII dress, a grey fedora and a woollen coat with only one tail over a satin doublet; but the doublet, the fedora and the coat were in a range of silvery greys, like the moon, a portrait which seemed to have been painted with frost and steel and the pallor of mother-of-pearl, a pearl amid all this moiré; the face was charmingly pale and sad, a good-natured, energetic face with large eyes, devouring, burning, and resigned.

Long blue-black curls obscured the white face; a large guipure lace collar lengthened the neck's attachment to the body; on the already faded lips there was a smile of infinite lassitude; behind the mysterious face, an autumn sky, a crepuscular sky inflamed with reddish waves. That was the whole portrait.

A viscount of Applaincourt, my old cousin had told me one day when I caught her on the harpsichord, the harpsichord that she would never open, but which she had opened that day and where she was lingering, seated, her fingers magnetically attracted to the keys, her eyes on the panelling, the panelling where the appealing face would not reveal itself to me until years later, but which was insignificant to me on that day.

A viscount of Applaincourt! Applaincourt, the mournful majestic chateau of the eleventh century lost in a swamp and some reedy fields; Applaincourt, where under Henri III the league of Flanders was signed.

My old cousin couldn't have known this viscount; he was already dead for two centuries before she was even born, the handsome knight decked in watered silk and glimmers, and yet I have since become convinced that if Mademoiselle Olympe d'Estournelle did not marry, and died a canoness, it was because of that handsome portrait or at the very least because of a resemblance with the man in the portrait.

And since that time, on the luminous grey days of autumn, when nature, exceedingly weary and stripped of her colours, seems to put on satin and moiré, when here and there she wads herself in fog, with purple tints in the trees and steely gleams on the still water, then it's the portrait of the man in my cousin's room which reappears before me. It reappears in its silvery greys with its resigned, haughty face, summarising like a synthesis the aching sadness of the year, the fading light of the beautiful days that are passing and the enveloping sweetness of days long gone.

And I can hear a sound like the rustling of reed-cutting.

Jean Lorrain was the pseudonym of Paul Duval (1855-1906), a French author and judgmental spectator of Belle Époque decadence. He was renowned for his flamboyant homosexuality and an addiction to ether. Though admired in his lifetime for his literary achievements, many feared him for his caustic humour and journalistic attacks on leading figures. Lorrain had a taste for the morally distasteful, which was an expression of his hatred of the masks and morals of his era. Critics have often focused on his eccentricities at the expense of his works, which portray his society and its obsessive fears. Though much of his writing remains unread today, even in French, he rewards study, for many of his stories question our prejudices, leaving the reader unmasked and uneasy.

Patricia Worth has a Master of Translation Studies from the Australian National University. Her translation of George Sand's *Spiridion* was published in 2015, and two bilingual short story books from New Caledonia were published in 2017 and 2018. A number of her translations have appeared in Australian, New Caledonian and US literary journals including *Southerly Journal*, *Transnational Literature*, *The Brooklyn Rail* and *Delos Journal*.

Erin-Claire Barrow is an author and illustrator originally from the Adelaide Hills in South Australia. She paints in watercolours to create whimsical scenes, storybook illustrations, and bring to life the strange creatures of fairy tales and folklore. Erin-Claire is always on the lookout for ways to combine her passions for art and equality, and is particularly interested in how art can be used to raise awareness of social justice issues.

www.ingramcontent.com/pod-product-compliance
Lightning Source LLC
Chambersburg PA
CBHW070511170726
48291CB00008B/2701